DELIBERATELY DISOBEYING DADDY

BY
AIYSHA SWALLOWGREN

ISBN 979-8-9878596-0-5
First Printing February 2023
Printed in United States of America

Contents

A Bit

She's reading my words and the are making her a bit
Wet but no panties today leaving a puddle where she sits
There are so many strange men groping her, rubbing her clit
She's swallowed so much cum it's easy to forget
So many strangers, she's a filthy used cumdump and in a bit
We're going to fuck her really hard, we don't give a shit
If it hurts because more pain really wets her hot slit
She's the greediest cumslut, she would never spit
It out good girl lick all the cum off your slutty outfit
I love making her pussy super wet, more than a bit
When she gets choked, slapped, chained, roughly hit
It makes her crave for more spitroasts the gang will split
Her in two I'm slapping her ass with a leather whip
Using my fingers, sticking them in her mouth here sip
Our cum whore she was happy to totally commit
To being a well-used filthy, nasty cumbucket
You're a filthy fuckdoll now slap your tit
Is this making it wet, perhaps a bit?

APART

She asks me to widely tear her apart
She is being naughty so she will start
Touching her most sensitive, hottest part
Together we make such sensational art
The flame inside, my emotions, tear her apart
She's so turned on when I share my heart
Her hands so hotly begin to dart
Grabbing and rubbing herself from how smart
I am, my vulnerability tears her insides apart
I'm whispering things to help jumpstart
Her desires, she's getting so hot, she's coming apart

ASKING

I always feel comfortable with her asking
If I would admire her some more so she can start basking
In my warmth, the heat has her gasping
It's a slow, passionate burn and it keeps lasting
I can always be totally myself, never masking
My emotions and I start slowly asking
If I can inspire her to start grasping
Her tight body as her hands start unclasping
Her bra she creates temptations that are everlasting
I want to blow her mind so I start blasting
Her with sweetness, is this good for you I keep asking

Assist

Let me lead you deep into temptation, let me assist
You by whispering things too hot to resist
You're a fiery, lustful, wild hedonist
You touch your rose more than any botanist
Your mind is now racing, as I continue to assist
You with sensual thoughts that always persist
You should relax, lay back, receive, I insist
You are fully in the moment, opening your gift
You make me forget fear, or that I have a lisp
I want you to embrace pleasure, feel a swift
Rise in your temperature allow me to uplift
You which makes your skirt start to lift
I'm making it hotter just like you wished
I'm tonguing your most sensitive spots and kissed
Your ass, when you listen to me you start using your wrist

ATTENTION

Nothing gets her going like tons of attention
She loves the feeling of so many hungry men
Staring at her especially the type of gentleman
That knows just how to make her grin
I'm giving her desires my full attention
Finally a man that knows how to listen
I want to make you sweat, make you glisten
All I can think of is eating you out on a mission
To make you squirt everywhere especially when
You let several guys finger you I should
Mention that I've brought several friends
We're here to make sure you get undivided attention
Does that make you start leaking as I slide in your DMs?

BEAST MODE

Sometimes she tries provoking me into beast mode
She wanted to be taken right there on the side of the road
As people watched she continued and she rode
Me until she was a quivering puddle, she loves beast mode
Her favorite thing is when I fully explode
On her face, in her mouth I took pictures and showed
Them to my girlfriend I've got a boatload
Of ways to make her hot as I unload
On her again she finished recording and started to upload
Another nasty film as my cum slowly flowed
Out of her I hot slow-mo and watching it leaked slowed
Down is getting me right back into beast mode

BEAUTIFUL SUNSET

I woke her up after she had been quite upset
I whispered you're prettier than a beautiful sunset
My sweetness quickly made her forget
Anything else she said I've never met
Someone that compared me to a beautiful sunset
I told her lay back and she laid down and let
Me start licking her legs until she's dripping wet
My lip service is really making her sweat
She lets me use her body, she's my palette
Making her feel so good she'll never forget
How it feels to feel prettier than a beautiful sunset

BEGINNER

If you'd let me continue being a beginner
Begin again she utters with a whimper
I'm your butterfly, my fluttering makes you quiver
Encouraging you to shine, drinking your shimmer
Tastes like heaven, my heavenly dinner
This is just the beginning, I'm a beginner
I want to make your face red and your eyes bigger
Make you bounce up and down like Pooh's friend Tigger
My lip service makes you feel thinner
Reading this makes you start using your finger
Cascades of rainbow waterfalls I'm a swimmer
I'm drowning in your pleasure pool as if I'm a beginner

BEHIND

She's rubbing herself wishing I'd get behind
Her my strength is her favorite kind
I'm making her drip as I start to grind
My strength against her she finds
It so hot when I push into her behind
I do things to her body and to her mind
I get her going, I really wind
Her up as our bodies slowly intertwine
The effect of her on me is genuine
I love squeezing into tight spaces, she's resigned
Herself to being totally taken from behind

BEND

My words inspire her to start to bend
In interesting ways she took a pic and hit send
I stir her insides by how I carefully blend
Naughty and sweet, she doesn't pretend
To be turned on she just starts to bend
She loves showing off her cute rear end
I am lifting her pleasure, she starts to ascend
My tongue starts to flick her and when I extend
It to her thighs slowly and carefully I spend
My energy as she stretches even further to bend

BIG MEN

She came up to me and said mmmm I like big men
I think she wants me to forcefully wipe the grin
Off her face being rough gets her hot deep within
She likes when I use my boy to helplessly pin
Her being put in her place by big men
Makes her drown in desires, she loves sin
When I grab her by the throat is the time when
She gets especially heated, she's rubbing herself again
She begs me to cum all over her face and chin
I'm going to do that now and when
She's covered fully she melts, she loves big men

BLOWHOLE

She's got the hottest holes, especially her blowhole
She wants all the dicks, she'll fuck the whole
Football team glad to be a dripping cum covered hole
She's a cheap, filthy cumbucket in her soul
You dear are such a gushing, filthy blowhole
You enjoy catching each drop in your mixing bowl
One in your mouth, one in your pussy, one in your asshole
Men blowing their loads all over your face filthy blowhole
I'm making your slutty parts leak, you can't control
Yourself you are swallowing all the cum you stole
Load after load as it leaked out and you hold
Two dicks in your hands while cum covers your face nasty blowhole

BREAK

Two naughty little vixens need a study break

They sit in my lap and start to shake

Julia Shoves her toy down Bella's throat, she can take

It deep and the moans are loud and not fake

I grab them by the hair and start to make

Them go down on each other now my snake

Is stimulated watching Julia and Bella's cake

Making each other vibrate, nasty little earthquakes

They are having a slumber party so I wake

Them up by warming my meat, they love steak

When I'm done with them they'll need a long break

Breakable

Dear darling unicorn you are so swift and breakable
The rougher I get the more your resolve becomes unstable
Filthy fucking animal that's on your name label
I'll fuck the hay out of you in a stable
I'm breaking you in properly, you're so breakable
You can't control your urges, you're unable
To stop touching yourself under the table
I know how to break you, I'm most capable
Putting you in weird positions that are inescapable
There's only one person here that's easily able
To break you with one blow, you're so breakable

BURNING

I'm creating a passionate wildfire that starts burning
Making her drip with anticipation and yearning
She's going the distance and she's learning
That fire can really ignite when I start turning
Her on even more it's making her feel burning
Desires and my tongue keeps concerning
Itself with putting out the fire by returning
Her heat now together we start burning
I'm in her mind and have her squirming
In her seat as my tongue keeps performing
Acrobatics to inspire more sensational burning

CHAIN

She was a nasty cumbucket so I took a chain
Tied her to a tree and started to explain
You have one job slut, you're hear to drain
All the dicks, we are running a train
On you my cumdump slave try to contain
Your excitement slut, you love the chain
Man after man sprays on you rapidly like opening champagne
You're such a nasty used cumbucket it's quite plain
To me that what you really desire is for me to restrain
You as I look at the line of men that remain
It's a good thing you like being choked by your chain
More cum sir, please sirs, I'm sticking my candy cane
In her ass then in her mouth she loves how my brain
Works and how I make her wet enough to exclaim
Cover me sirs with your cum, make it rain
That's what I'm good for, licking her cum covered chain

CHAMPAGNE FROM HEAVEN

Her soul was sipping on this champagne from heaven
I knew just what to say to really redden
Her face now here's an interesting question
Has anyone given her mental orgasms in quick succession
Be an awful student and I'll really teach you a lesson
Slowly her inhibitions and clothing start to lessen
She's always desired a non-stop succession
Of delight like sipping champagne from heaven
Her ass and face combined could cure clinical depression
I push her touching herself to a new level of obsession
She's touching herself, sliding things out and in
Tastes her fingers, tastes like champagne from heaven

CHEAP

She's a nasty little cumbucket that loves to be beat
She's a total gangbang slut, she loves dick deep
In her hot holes being used like a cheap
Whore really turns her on and makes her leak
She gobbles dick almost every day of the week
Letting everyone watch and join for cheap
You dear, you're a truly nasty piece of fuckmeat
You make my dick cry, it's starting to weep
All over your face as you use a bowl to collect a heap
Of sperm drink the bowl slut, enjoy your treat
Dick shoved down your throat as the cum starts to seep
Out of her well used holes she begged please keep
Using my holes I love feeling dirty and cheap

CLASSY

I only go places that are full of women that are classy
Which is wherever you dance the key
To communicating warmly is to be fun and sassy
A mixture of humble and very flashy
Darling you're my definition of classy
I hope my words stick to your mind like taffy
I want to make your body sing happily
Playing something smooth, something jazzy
You crave intelligent men that are savvy
Treating you with respect makes you happily
Start dancing you love when men are super classy

CLAY

I'm a passionate artist and you are clay
So well sculpted, you get more beautiful each day
There's something very unique about the way
That you bring out the very best of me when you display
That dazzling, sparkling smile always takes my breath away
That body of yours mesmerizing me as you sway
Flowing smoothly as my hands are in the clay
Molding you as we connect and you convey
How being a piece of art and the light which I portray
You in that makes you relax and start to lay
Back as I'm slowly wetting your entranceway
You loves as my hands glide expertly in the clay

COVER

In spite of my best efforts she continues to cover
I'm in her ear whispering let me help you discover
Waves of pleasure and then another
I want to be in your treasure and start to plunder
When you touch yourself I start to wonder
What's deeper inside you, you don't need to cover
Let my hands caress you as your undercover
Creator striking your body like lightning and I the thunder
Rumbles inside you, giving you a ravenous hunger
Your hands are starting to creep under
Your clothes, ass you start to tremble and shudder
Let me give you pleasure like no other
Man, let me see beneath you cover

CREATOR

She calls me her sensual, sexy creator
I know how to make her pleasure even greater
To her needs and desires I happily cater
To them as her hand goes below her equator
I'm creating shuddering shivering, I'm her creator
She's touching herself now, she'll continue later
Reading my words makes her a horny masturbater
She enjoys how I am such a loving communicator
For her I am bold and brave like a gladiator
Her body is the canvas to this creator

CRYSTAL

She dazzles everywhere, shining with beauty as clear as crystal
I want her to think of me making her sizzle
Letting her lust drip, my words start to drizzle
She desires to give into temptation, more than just a little
Firm, tone, she's built for fun, she's not brittle
Imagining that on our date she starts to pull
Down her panties rubbing her favorite crystal
Things to compliment her about there are a bucketful
I want her to start licking and biting her lips until
She can't take it anymore her hips start to swivel
She's definitely getting more interested, it's official
Is this warming you up, am I lighting up your crystal?

DECENT

She said angels were watching so she must be decent
Now the angels are starting to descent
They could smell from heaven, her scent
When she showers angels watch how frequent
She has to be sneaky and try to be a little decent
There's another angel, made out of cement
Another angel that she made pitch a tent
She's thinking of dressing like a nun, sneaking into a convent
Another angel lost its wings today when she bent
Over and God said damn, that's more than decent

DESTROY

I'm wrecking her concentration, starting to destroy
Her desires she's not innocent or coy
She loves most to be my well used toy
Nothing warms her more, fills her with more joy
Than when I use my size to overpower and destroy
Her body as my hands around her neck start to deploy
Her depravity she screams you're such a naughty boy
I beat her senseless and use her roughly, she truly enjoys
When I talk about fucking her like a rabbit in Playboy
She's on a crusade for pleasure like Helen of Troy
She's burning hot with desire, fire always destroys
Everything in its path, she's riding me like a cowboy
Everything I do is a well thought out ploy
To erase her inhibitions, give into temptation, let me destroy

Dew

I'm making her wetter than the morning dew
She reads my words and starts slipping into
Something more comfortable as she lost a few
Articles of clothing and I painted it drew
Her in making her damper than morning dew
She showed me herself whispering look what you do
To me as she couldn't resist the way I blew
Her mind with creativity, I've got a few
Ideas of ways to make her bite and chew
Her hot lips as her desires hotly grew
She's never gotten this hot, this is new
Refreshing and wetter than the morning dew

DISPLAY

She's a stunning work of art and she's on display
She becomes red and whispers the way
That you make me inspires me, makes me want to play
So I suggested she bend and move her hands away
Now her stunning canvas is on full display
She's shaking her hips and she starts to sway
I start licking her mind like it's the last day
Ever now my tongue, my muscular tongue displays
Creativity as I encourage her to slowly lay
Down and lower herself onto she doesn't weigh
Much but she's as hot as the sun's ray
My beautiful rainbow is dazzling on full display

Dragon Queen

I desire to ignite a fire deep within the Dragon Queen
To excite her mind and get a clear green
Light to elaborate on the fun and obscene
Things I'd like to do to her to make a scene
I want her fire, let me in dear Dragon Queen
Let me create a desire in you by licking you clean
And dirty and everything in between
I love when you bend over, you look lean
I hope reading these words on your screen
Make you feel youthful, like a teen
Let me really perk you up like caffeine
I hope you'll let my tongue be a machine
Making you hotter than hell as I apply sunscreen
Allow me to be of service, dear Dragon Queen

DUMPSTER

She's really, really trashy like a dumpster
Going deep in her mind with no rubber
She's had way more than a few lovers
But she's always ready to add another
You can take her right behind a dumpster
When I call her a filthy slut it really warms her
She loves being used in a dirty gutter
Especially by a very bad man, a bad motherfucker
She's a naughty student and I'm her firm instructor
She begs for more dick pretty please sir
Bring some friends and use me as your cum dumpster

ENERGETIC

She is openly receiving my pulses so energetic
I admire her tone body, it's so athletic
She's drawn towards my body, I'm magnetic
We are experimenting with a theoretic
Connection as she absorbs even more energetic
Vibes together we are quite synergetic
She's feeling her body tingle as I touch her kinesthetic
Channel giving her pleasures so epic
She's my nurse and I'm her paramedic
Reviving her, shocking her, I'm electric

Erotic Novel

It got her excited the way he wrote her an erotic novel
More cum sir she begs and starts to grovel
She's such a used cumdump her holes are full an awful
Lot she wants all the cum, she's the slut known as colossal
Her is a story about her, a short erotic novel
She sucks so many bones her lipstick tastes like a fossil
Her face and body covered by strangers' firehose nozzles
Her Eyelashes covered in cum she starts to bobble
On another dick, she's made to work in a brothel
Dirtiest hole would suck and fuck Jesus and all twelve apostles
All the dicks, all her hot holes filled as she gobbles
More and more dick, it's an ever-expanding erotic novel

EXPERIMENT

She gladly agreed to my interesting experiment
No man had ever tried to truly augment
Her mind and the words that I just sent
Made her hot and heavy, she could smell her scent
She needed to be explored one hundred percent
I told her to bend over and she was compliant
Now we are exploring spankings in this experiment
If I let her use my hand, if I lent
Her my fingers she'd suck on them going silent
As I awaken the beast within, all her pent
Up energy as I move her body into perfect alignment
I'm helping her experience new levels of excitement
We're having fun doing a sexy experiment

FLOWER

Regardless of circumstances the rose will still flower
Giving its beauty to all every hour
That passes it goes from sweet to sour
Letting what unfolds start causing the wildflower
To spread joy, it will always flower
One thing about the connection we have our
Feelings may be hurt but we use our brainpower
To find a princess locked high in a tower
The sweetest words I send to empower
You dear rose, you are a most stunning flower

FOREVER

She asked if she could save it and keep it forever
Be a naughty student and I'll be your professor
Nobody had made her holes this hot ever
My hands slap her pretty face and increase the pressure
Around her neck, she's a cumbucket of pleasure
I'd like to bottle your juices and measure
Out shots drink your juices, drink cum forever
You are flexible, freaky, so let me use my clever
Nature to tickle your clit with a peacock feather
There's flurries of cum on her, that's my forecast for the weather
She loves when I tie my belt around her neck strong leather
Love watching you and your slut friends get facialized together
Can I keep making your hot holes wetter and wetter
She is the filthiest fucking whore, always and forever

FOUND

I went looking for pleasure and I found
Her there making the cutest sound
She was grasping the hottest, round
Parts and was definitely not messing around
I took the hot cat to the playground
I've found my muse, my muse is found
When she licks her lips I become spellbound
I'm using my tongue on her hot mound
She's releasing her essence, all that wound
Up energy I called her queen and crowned
Her at last my lovely lady is found

FULL

Your beautiful lips are so wonderfully full
Bringing you in closer as you start to pull
At my pants grabbing a naughty handful
I want to make you know that you're truly beautiful
I want to fill you with sweetness, you're so full
Of joy and delight let us act like you are in school
You're opening your legs in a roomful
Of people in your seat a liquid starts to pool
You grab a banana and start to suck and drool
Feed me your nectar, your juices are my fuel
Nothing is better than when your mouth becomes full

GLAM

This is about the sexy, sophisticated , and very glam
Model that shows her body on Onlyfans
I'm talking about you, you mam
You're a stone cold fox and you're so damn
Pretty your picture is in the dictionary under glam
I think of your body like an exotic land
I'd like to explore you body on black sand
Put sunscreen on you perhaps my hand
Would wander I'm wondering if perhaps I can
Make your day hot, even hotter than
Before dear can I help you expand
Your definition of pleasure I truly understand
The effect of you on my waistband
You're so fucking sexy, you're so glam

GOAT

She's my favorite cumslut, super talented throat goat
She feels in her place with cock shoved down her throat
Tears of happiness down her cheek as she again deepthroats
My dick she's getting excited from the things I wrote
I want to facefuck you, there's no need to sugarcoat
It if we were voting best side piece she'd get my vote
Making love to dick with her mouth is her favorite thing to devote
Herself to so much drooling and spit you may need a raincoat
Be my naughty secretary and make me start to promote
You drowning in cum but you don't need a lifeboat
You'll swallow it all down, my thirsty little goat

GOING

Slowly and surely I'm getting her thoughts going
Her appetite and desire for temptation keeps growing
She's imagining my tongue as it's slowing
Down right on the edges of her opening
The hotter I get the more she starts glowing
It's making her slowly start disrobing
I can see the effect on her body, she's going
Crazy touching herself, pleasure puddles start flowing
Like a butterfly I'm flicking my tongue and blowing
Her mind she's imagining me throwing
Her like a doll, it makes her start overflowing
I'm making her smile as I keep showing
Her new levels of pleasure, it really gets her going

GRATEFUL

She was always available and always grateful
For my touch, my big hands are able
To take her at anytime, she finds herself unable
To stop touching herself reading my messages she's grateful
Started off sweet, slowly forcing her to do things painful
She dreams of me fucking her doggy doing deep anal
She's not a princess and this isn't a fable
But when it comes to nastiness I really enable
Her dirtiest side she's tied up with some cable
I'm pounding her like I'm a stapler and she a staple
Spreading her lips she drenched her bagel
Eat your juices for breakfast slut, I know you're grateful

GYM

I dreamed about meeting you in the gym
You catch me staring, it makes you really grin
Looking at your beautiful hair, you're so thin
You are deliberately bending over in front of me again
I come up to you and say your body's built for sin
She invites me in the locker room and in the gym
She starts hovering on top of me and starts to spin
I'm touching the naughtiest parts of her deep within
I'm licking her neck, she really loves when
She gets attention she loves feeling the eyes of many men
On her today as she's on a naughty mission
I'm giving her goosebumps, she can feel her skin
Being stimulated and she's moaning as I slide in
Her it gets her so heated when she does it at the gym

HOMEWRECKER

She loves being a side piece, she's a really huge homewrecker
She enjoys being a filthy, nasty cumbucket she said sir
I'll be sloppy, blowing spit bubbles I'm better
At sucking dick than your wife and it gives me pleasure
To be on my knees servicing taken men this homewrecker
Likes being facefucked and this is my love letter
You use your head quickly, bobbing faster than a woodpecker
Being the only one they cheat with fills her
With glee as her saliva drips down her sweater
She enjoys being a piece of fuckmeat, she's a true beggar
Please cheat with me, you deserve a huge homewrecker
As she starts worshipping and swallowing another pecker
She enjoys facefucking in the woods, she's a go getter
Calling her names while using her holes get her wetter
She's turned on by being a slut, she loves being a homewrecker

HONEY

There are so many things to admire about you little bunny
You're so bright, warm, heavenly, and sunny
You ling for sweet words and jokes that are funny
My words on you mind are sweeter than honey
I slowly tease your mind to fill you with glee
I'm making you very heated and a little runny
Running your hands slowly between your knee
You're desperate to touch yourself, you feel free
To make yourself boil over like hot tea
I'm making you feel so heated especially
When you savor my sweetness, tastes like honey

HONEY 1

She sent a hot little video and asked honey
How does it get hotter than you dear sunny
I meant how can I get sunny hotter what's funny
Is that most men act like a total dummy
I prefer making her drip like honey
In her ear whispering something smutty
I want to make you leak everywhere, so runny
Sunny is in my hands and I mold her like putty
She's reading this and feeling so slutty
I'm warming her up like the sun does to honey

INSPIRATION

Writing today to tell you I'm grateful for inspiration
You're one of the most beautiful creatures in all creation
When you think about me I hope it's the warmest sensation
You're sensational and I thought what was motivational
To you and realized gratitude for inspiration
In your mind I'm licking your favorite location
I love delivering and exceeding your expectations
You love when I whisper give into temptation
Let me touch you I ways that create admiration
Fill your mind and body with colorful animation
I want to be on your mind, ruining your concentration
Thank you my naughty vixen, my best inspiration

INSPIRATIONS

She started showing her world for birthday inspirations
I said surrender to all your desires, to all temptations
Why fight the feelings, give in to all the sins
Imagine my tongue doing circular rotations
Giving your body new levels of divine inspiration
You're feeling so hot and the sensations
Keep coming, I'm using my tongue shaking great vibrations
My tongue is an artist with careful applications
Of naughty inspired by you, you create many inspirations

INTENTION

She feels as if I am right beside her, which is the intention
When I whisper things to her I always hotly mention
That I'm touching her on all cylinders like an engine
I take the time to ask things and carefully listen
Connection, deep connection is my intention
Also I truly enjoy making her glisten
The way she hangs on my words with rapt attention
Like she's a naughty schoolgirl and in detention
She likes my creativity and my original invention
Makes her so lustful, it fills her with sin
Delicious warmth spreading over her body is my intention

JESSIE

I wanted to tell you something Jessie
I've met a lot of women and have a bevy
Of mermaid friends that say undress me
I know just how to make you start breathing heavy
When she reads this, she touches herself, Jessie
Dear I'm going to make you very messy
I'll make you sparkly more than Elvis Pressley
You've got cute, tiny tits, you're not chesty
But that butt well it's so heavenly
When I excite your intimate, hot, fleshly,
Parts I know exactly what I'm doing to Jessie
Making her leak hotly, freely, effortlessly

KEN

She called me Barbie and she wants to be Ken
I always am sweet and make her grin
I know how to make her smile again and again
You're so fucking naughty, the definition of sin
If you want to fuck Barbie well then
That means you want to stick something in
Me and I say bring a hot friend
She needs spankings so she starts to bend
Over my knee I'm Barbie and she's Ken
She wants to be only one type of friend
Friends with benefits she touches herself when
She thinks about playing dress up, she loves to pretend
I want to lick your super hot, tight Argentinian
Body giving you naughty deep within
She really loves fucking Barbie, just like Ken

KEY

I was finding the right combination, the key
To ignite her passions so vividly
I tell her that when she shares it helps free
My imagination to find new ways to touch herself pleasantly
I'm making her feel so good the heavenly
Feelings and sensations flow effortlessly
She's starting to reach in between her knee
As she starts flowing like the tide does to the sea
I'm a locksmith and I definitely have the key
To open her starting to fill with glee
Between the two of us the intimacy
We share makes me start feeling so beastly
She's a blooming rose, and I'm a bumblebee
Helping her rose bloom so brilliantly
I excite her mind, body, and soul, that's the key

KISS HERE

Her new tattoo said kiss here
So I told her to bring the camera near
So I could better look, even leer
Her body makes mine fill with cheer
I want to see you cheerlead as I kiss here
Let me kiss you slowly and softly dear
Let me make you smile and have a happy tear
Pull that bodysuit to the side, show your rear
Even more so I can start to kiss here

LIFT

She started playfully starting to lift
Her shirt no bra, what an amazing outfit
I want to make you slowly start to sit
On my lap and let me unwrap my gift
You like the effect it has on me so you start to lift
Even more and you're making me shift
Dripping desires flood your mind so swift
Let me raise your temperature, let me uplift
Your pleasures washing over you like a snowdrift
When it comes to you, I definitely wished
You to continue, I love when you lift

MARILYN

She's the second coming of sexbomb, a sultry Marilyn
She enjoys when I make her hot, especially when
I tell her open you mind and I'll put my fingers in
Your mouth, you're tasting yourself, licking hot sin
She wants to be the naughtiest man, most men
Don't know how to speak properly to a Marilyn
Her body can't help leaking when I begin
Elaborating giving her goosebumps all over her skin
She's curvy, horny as fuck, I'm putting my balls on her chin
Helping her embrace the nastiest whore deep within
She asks for me to beat it up again and again
I'm throwing her against the wall, using her like a mannequin
Being a naughty, filthy pervert makes her body sing like a violin
Play with yourself hotly, fucking touch yourself Marilyn!

MESSING

She said she was just fucking with me a little messing
I'm here thinking of the best way to make her so effing
Excited that she can't help but to start caressing
Herself as she eagerly and quickly starts undressing
I'm messing in between her legs and it's getting
Very hot her panties are toast she's messing
Them up and onto my lap she starts pressing
Her hot little body on top of mine she's confessing
To secretly loving all three holes filled I'm addressing
That desire she's excited and starts forgetting
She's in public she's stripping and letting
Everyone watch her hot holes get used she's petting
Herself as I help her really get started messing

Mi Amor

The hottest woman whispering mi amor
I'm in between her thighs giving her pure
Deliciousness as I make her body pour
Juices my tongue knows how to ensure
That she keeps screaming mi amor
She's a hungry jaguar and I make her roar
With delight she loves how I sweetly adore
Her and how devoted I am to her pleasure
When I say she's prettier than any shell on the shore
Of Maui dear do you know what you're
Doing to me, you're so sexy mi amor

MIND

There she was dressed so fancy, blowing my mind
She keeps getting fancier, sexier, and more refined
She said if you let all your barriers down you'll find
That I'm a ton of fun when I relax and unwind
I love your fancy flower dress as much as your mind
She enjoyed a mixture of naughty and kind
You're so beautiful and that dress well designed
Each time I see you, elegance becomes redefined
I did my best to make my punchline well timed
How does it get better than her firm behind
It gets better when she starts to bump and grind
Intoxicating, exhilarating, you're sublime
Is this touching to you, deep in your mind?

MIRACULOUS

The art and inspiration she provides is miraculous
She loved being my muse, I worship her fabulous
Everything which helps her forget about bashfulness
I study her body and find superior elaborateness
The effect of my words on her body is miraculous
She's super naughty doing things most scandalous
Anything for my words, I've done an analysis
On the best way to fill her with ampleness
'The way I speak sweetly increases my handsomeness
I bring out the beast in her, she's a hungry lioness
She's trying to inhale my whole maleness
Taking it all in her hot, pretty mouth, how miraculous

MORE AND MORE

She loved when I continued pounding more and more
Firmly and with great power I helped restore
Her desires, her needs, her cravings throwing her on the floor
Dragging her by her hair like a nasty fucking whore
She loves my depravity, how I keep getting more and more
Fierce on her ass, her juices are starting to pour
As my hands roughly and quickly explore
New, exciting ways to get her sore
Lifting her by her neck, throwing her against the door
I'm sticking my fingers in, I've already got four
Inside and I'm going to keep pushing more and more

NECKING

I'm focusing on your mind, I'm checking
In to whisper things that I'm betting
That your neck is getting red, you are necking
Continue I can see your eyes beckoning
Me to encourage you to start forgetting
All barriers it feels so good temptation is letting
You go to new places as my tongue starts petting
Your brain and my lips slowly start pecking
I'm drinking your essence as you start sweating
Right into your naughty mind, that's where this is heading
Nothing is hotter than when you start begging
I'm taking you to the edge repeatedly, I'm edging
You closer and closer licking your neck I'm wetting
Your desires, good morning, here's some hot necking

NECTAR

She's a little, shiny hummingbird and I'm her nectar
She shows me her entire body, I'm her inspector
She's keeping all of my poems, she's a collector
When she starts letting me guide and play director
I'm using my mouth to savor her nectar
I make her feel safe, I'm an excellent protector
Not parent or preacher, never do I lecture
We're molding together in a rainbow connector
Making her flower bloom with lots of pleasure
Savoring her divine essence, sipping her nectar

New Favorite

I'm making her holes hot with a new favorite
The more I degrade her, the more I spit
On her face the wetter it makes her slit
She loves dicks so much she's a cumdump, a bottomless pit
She loves when I squeeze and roughly slap her tits
I'm in her ear whispering a new favorite
She's enjoying her holes stretching, she is able to fit
Four fingers inside herself how nasty can you get
I'm focusing on using my tongue on your clit
You're taking so many bananas an they start to split
You while spit roasting you so roughly you'll never forget
I like your whoreish Brittany Spears schoolgirl outfit
You love being a cheap thrill, a fucktoy, you openly admit
That you'd love to take me in your mouth and submit
To being a piece of fuckmeat I will permit
You to touch yourself with four fingers, your new favorite

OFFEND

You make me want to dive into the shallow end
When I ask for what I desire and you won't send
Anything, not even a cute bend
I am just a man, I admire your rear end
I won't hold anything back and if I should offend
Just remember that we can always start over again
Do you not see me as a lover, more as a friend
All the vulnerable things I've penned
Trying to make the hottest, naughtiest blend
To warm you up it's never my intention to offend

OVERHEAT

She asked specifically for me to make her overheat
I know how to do it, I have a trick that's neat
Slowly sucking, licking, nibbling her feet
As I move higher I can feel her heat
I can also see the puddle collecting in her seat
I roughly grab her tits, she loves how I beat
Them and she tries sticking all of my meat
In her mouth as she starts to overheat
She loves how I mix naughty and sweet
Expertly and how I easily lift her like an athlete
On our first date we are heading to the backseat
I'm going to do my best to overeat
Her as my tongue and her body meet
It's getting sizzling, she's continuing to overheat

Passion

She's quite talented and her enthusiasm and passion
For sucking dick making being a slut the new fashion
She opens her drooling mouth and starts to unfasten
My pants she needs breakfast, cum fed to her as I ration
Out my seed she's so greedy for it and her passion
For being a throat goat and a well used receptacle, a cum bin
She's choking as it goes deeper, it makes her grin
When she gets facefucked she keeps gagging again and again
Her mouth is being stretched, her holes are built for sin
She enjoys being a slut in front of a ton of men
She's in tune with the nastiest whore deep within
Herself sticking it deep down her throat with passion
There's spit all over her body, she's covered her skin
What a filthy fucking whore as I spray her mouth and chin
She keeps bobbing her head and her tongue begins to spin
Please use me like a piece of fuckmeat, she begs with passion

Perfect Guy

She was hoping to finally meet the perfect guy
The type that makes her leak down her thigh
Someone that enjoys the fact that she is bi
She needs a firm hand to remind her why
Her ass hurts sliding in is the perfect guy
She's playful and decides to try
To disobey but I smack her like a fly
Choking the breath out of her, looking in her eye
Being totally dominated makes her cry
In joy as he knows how much force to apply
Lifting her like a doll, I hear her start to sigh
She will be disciplined until she begins to comply
Taking off my belt I grab her neck and tie
It tight, she's getting destroyed by her perfect guy

Pie

Turning her on is as easy as pie
She's smoking a bowl, getting really high
I've not got a first born to sacrifice but let me try
To turn up the heat and make her leak down her thigh
I invited a hundred men to cum into this pie
She is ready to eat it all she said why
Don't you just start to unzip your fly
And join the gang that's starting to multiply
The cum is caked thick on her body, not an inch is dry
All the dicks, all the cum, she's so happy she could cry
When it comes to nasty she needs an infinite supply
To get in her gangbang I would happily crucify
Jesus Christ she gives me wood I don't even need to buy
A cross, I'm scrambling your guts so hot it starts to liquify
I want to look directly at her, eye to eye
I heard you were a cumbucket let me verify
That by overfilling you with my creampie
She's fingering herself quicker than a butterfly
As she eats another slice of cum filled pie

PLEASED

She loved to be admired, it really pleased
Her so she bent over further and teased
Me as she slowly starts dropping to her knees
She knows how to get what she wants with ease
I'm making it so hot, the more pleased
She gets the more that I hotly breathed
On her neck with ideas she helped conceive
She's rubbing herself a lot, it eased
Her tension she loves how I perceive
Her body she'll do anything to make me pleased

PREPARE

She asked if I was ready and I said how can anyone prepare
For you being aggressive in just your underwear
I'm being bold, going where most men don't dare
Licking your mind, making your senses more aware
I don't think you are ready, I have started to prepare
A seat for you, use my face as your chair
I say the raciest things with plenty of flair
Lowering you inhibitions, all is laid bare
You like feeling so warmly embrace by your teddy bear
I know how ot make you start shaking by grabbing your hair
I'm ready now and forcefully start to tear
Off your lingerie now you are damp as I scare
You for the beast within and you swear
You thought you were ready, but you didn't prepare

PRIME

She deserved treats so I ordered from Amazon Prime

Things that will do things to her mind

I'm like a fat cock thrusting into her behind

She said I could rap this out it's so well rhymed

I'll do anything to get her juices working overtime

Reading my words just before bedtime

Making her so creamy, filthy unicorn slime

Leaks down her leg, her well is starting to prime

Her hot flower is opening like springtime

I whisper the hottest things to her at nighttime

I want to make her cum the hardest in her lifetime

I've got a snack for you dear, it's mealtime

You're licking me everywhere horny little feline

You've got the horniest, nastiest holes, they're Grade A Prime

RAILED

Sometimes she got the urge to just get railed
I am happy to oblige as I make her passions sail
She wanted to be hammered, desperate to get nailed
I'm grabbing her by her pretty ponytail
Just beating it up totally, she loves getting railed
She tried to not touch herself but she failed
In between her legs I warmly exhaled
Then back in deep as I hotly impaled
Her again until she screams and her body flailed
Being destroyed made her feel so hot, so female
Everywhere she sits leaves a damp trail
I finished inside her after I had railed

RAINBOW BACKSIDE

She said my art looks like the rainbow backside
Or the back of a rainbow I really tried
To contain myself but it's impossible to hide
You are colorful like a rainbow inside
Just for a minute can I help guide
You to relax ad come play slip and slide
All morning I've been thinking of your rainbow backside
You're so curvaceous I love making you smile wide
Your beautiful lips I like when your pleasure gets multiplied
Your hunger, your desires are becoming amplified
I want to do things to you that will remain classified
I'm climbing your beautiful mountainside
All I can dream of is making you very satisfied
My tongue is running up and down your rainbow backside

RECEPTIVE

Surrender all and become open and receptive
I'm here in your ear whispering things that give
You thrilling meltings by being so darn perceptive
I'm very slow, very patient, and receive directive
To go lower as your body is most receptive
To pleasure though beauty can be somewhat subjective
I'm making you go back to temptation and you relive
Out your wildest fantasies, I'm very selective
In how I warm you, making you so receptive

RIPPING

She wanted deep desires, the kind that get her ripping
Off her clothes and her spirits keep lifting
The more I say you're beautiful, the more it's hitting
Her right on her happy button, I want it dripping
For me your dress makes me want to start ripping
The straps off, I'm a big man and I'm spinning
You in circles making you laugh and start wildly grinning
I want you hanging on every word, start gripping
Yourself as I get it extra slick and glistening
Cover me in you juices, start christening
Me in holy water you're uncontrollably dripping
You're not just taking your panties off, you're roughly ripping

SCENT

I'm a very motivated beast and I'm tracking your scent
I can smell where you've been, you went
There again got you so heated you had to vent
Your neck is turning red and Joseph lent
Me his nose, went nose first in your scent
Joseph inhales heaven, it's raining heaven scent
Drops I want you to let out all that pent
Up desire like when Venus bent
Over causing me to pitch a tent
Inhaling Venus' essence makes me hard as cement
How does it get better that a dripping ribbon wrapped present
Licking Venus' inner thighs increasing the torment
I'm diving into temptation, she's starting to invent
New secretions on my face, I'm drinking Venus' scent

SENSUAL

Forgetting everything else, she embraces her sensual
Desires to do things with me most sinful
She loves to show me how tremendously flexible
She is by trying to fit both my testicles
In her small mouth, she's my hot receptacle
Being open to her body experiencing most sensual
Things will always lead to climax, the eventual
Conclusion as I take her to the pentacle
Of desire my words touching her like tentacles
If I was an octopus and had several
Limbs I would be even bolder, very sensual
Words of admiration for you I have a plentiful
Supply open your legs, make it more accessible
Let me feast on your delicious body, it's so delectable
Let me give you orgasms so unforgettable
By being so lovingly kind and sensual

SHIVERING

What I do to her body is incomprehensible, she's shivering
She needs passion so badly and I keep delivering
Things that make her insides sparkle and start shimmering
I get her very heated, it's almost blistering
Hot and yet her body starts to shake, she's shivering
She enjoys my mouth and how it's giving
Her wild ideas as my tongue starts flickering
Right there she can't help but to start fingering
Herself I've got her so heated she's simmering
She needs release so bad, I'm keeping her shivering

SHOWER

When she wakes up and starts recording her shower
With a banana in her mouth it's my favorite hour
Use you lips of Daddy, use your power
For good and creating hot little shower
Clips imagine it is me that you devour
As you bloom beautifully my flower
With your tongue ring igniting my brainpower
Use you body to help inspire and empower
Me I love seeing you in the shower

Sinful Lips

She remarked that I had very sinful lips
The better to taste you with as I slip
My hand under your dress and start to rip
Your panties being rough quickly makes you flip
Into a lustful, aggressive, horny devil swaying your hips
I take your throat firmly in my powerful grip
The other hand touching your sinful lips
I'm pinching and slapping your perky tits
You're leaking down your legs, your body starts to twitch
I know exactly what you need, you filthy fucking bitch
You're reading this and down your thigh drips
Desire you want me to kiss your sinful lips

SLOWER

A wise women taught me the power of going slower
She said let all your barriers down, and as I would lower
Them completely I'd practice vulnerability with her
I'd sow seeds of naughty and became an expert sower
The vibe is warm, delicious, and enhanced by going slower
Slowing it down for her lights her up like a flamethrower
It's her eyes that beckon me to mold her desires like a glassblower
Her body is like a gymnast, a runner, and a rower
Combined together and today I am taking the time to show her
The beauty she reflects as I continue to go even slower

SO BEAUTIFULLY

She says my art is so beautiful and I'm so beautifully
Touched I'm going to take down my walls usually
I start thinking of what else is possible and truthfully
You are fertilizer for my garden which fruitfully
Blooms with delicious ripeness so beautifully
You know just how to get my body singing musically
Wait I mean how is that beauty possible humanely
When you share your photos it's an opportunity
To dare and dream bigger, you inspire such ingenuity
I love when you wear fancy dresses and jewelry
You're decadent, luscious, and always shine so beautifully

SQUISHY

She is reading my words and getting very squishy
I'm putting her big ass over my knee
She surrenders to temptation, I know what she
Needs more than anything is to insert three
Fingers inside and quickly rub, make it super squishy
I'm licking her neck, firmly smacking her tushy
She tries to grab my dick, she's so pushy
She wants me deep in her mouth, then her pussy
Make it juicy for daddy, get it super squishy
I'm making her so heated, she loves when I'm super smutty
I'm buzzing around her flower like a bumblebee
She pinches her nipples roughly moaning nobody
Gets me as wet as you sir, you make it extra squishy

SUIT

She's showing off in her little pink suit
So many things in my mind start to shoot
I'd like to slowly taste your luscious fruit
Telling her how very sexy and cute
She is reaching her hand into the pants of her suit
Making her feel like lightning starts to shoot
Out of her body I'm licking her down to her root
Chakra my hands reaching down her jumpsuit
She's noticing I have started to salute
Her this is what happens from your pink suit

SWEAT

I always know how to make her sweat
To give her pleasure that she'll never forget
It gets better and better she can't help but pet
Herself as I constantly make her very wet
I'm whispering in her ear, I want you to sweat
Like never before as she remembers when my tongue met
Her sensitive spots and I have a unique mindset
She's my muse and her body is my palette
She's dripping everywhere, covered in sweat

SWIM

She let me dip in her pool and I started to swim
It brought out much joy, she's starting to grin
She knows what's coming, it's that time again
Time to go deeper in the pool, as I swim
I make sure that I'm covering every inch of every limb
There's overflow from her pool, it's filled to the brim
I'm working her out like we are at the gym
I whisper you're so curvy yet thin
It lights a raging fire deep within
Her as I beckon her to lay back and sin
I'm doing laps in her pleasure pool, I love to swim

TALENTED

You my dearest muse are so very talented
You paint my mind the fiercest red
I love watching you practice giving head
Thinking of me as you grab yourself in bed
You're simply the best, you're so talented
Open your mind and observe how your legs spread
You give me your nectar and as I fed
Her soul I massaged the neglected
Parts of her body, my tongue was unexpected
Now it's my turn to show her that I'm very talented

TENSION

I'm really building her excitement, I'm increasing the tension
My large hand around her throat keeps her attention
On doing nasty, filthy things she'd never mention
To anyone else and my words are creating dripping suspension
She's a horny little slut, calling her fuckmeat increases the tension
I'm doing things to touch her in ways that defy comprehension
She's rubbing herself rapidly into a new dimension
She's a naughty student who deserves detention
Showing her panties to me, she's ready for my newest invention
I take her right to the edge then slowly start the extension
Of my tongue on her thighs rapidly increasing the tension

Tone

She was checking out my legs, she likes tone
Men that make her mind race when she's alone
I pick her up, she smells my Aqua Di Gio cologne
She likes the racy things I write, she starts to moan
She wanted a firm, strong man with which to bone
She gets heated from my oolite and naughty tone
Making her feel like a priceless gemstone
Being respectful gets her heated in her erogenous zone
I want to take her to new levels of pleasure, the unknown
When men take the time to focus above her collarbone
She desires a strong, vulnerable man filled with testosterone
It order to get a better angle I put her on a throne
She loves excellent head, it makes her shake and groan
Is this hot enough for you baby, do you like my tone

Understood

There's something truly sexy about being understood
When I think of you I think of all the good
Things there are to admire and perhaps I should
Tell you that I never thought anyone could
Change my definition of beauty, I thought I understood
I looked at you twice thinking well would
You look at that little devil, she excites my manhood
I'm fixated on pleasing her and the likelihood
Of that increases the more she feels understood

Unique Read

She said my poetry is a very erotic, kinky unique read
She loves to swallow it all, she swallows cum with greed
She's a greedy cumslut and I know just what she needs
he needs to be used, she loves being used indeed
Touching herself to the hottest, raciest unique read
I want you to touch yourself with aggression and speed
Making her suck your juices her your anal beads
Filthiest fuckdoll begs for cum, she really pleads
For more dick, filling her hot mouth again with my seed
Come into temptation with me, let me lead
You to the nastiest places with another kinky unique read

UNUSUAL

She called me romantic and my words are unusual
Imagining I'm her banana makes my mind fruitful
You are really, really so beautiful
I love your skin, it is so youthful
Your body is my canvas, you're my fuel
You fuel desires, bringing out the unusual
Was yourself, rub yourself for hot renewal
Show me your naughty parts, your jewel
You make me so hot, it's cool
Let's make the hottest things, make it mutual
Let me make it so hot it's quite unusual

VERY INVITING

It's been said that my tongue is very inviting
I'm inviting you to brace yourself for very exciting
Things licking your lips as you can't help biting
She confesses to touching herself while reading my writing
I'm headed into temptation, it's very inviting
Imagine a while night spent delighting
It's impossible to resists, no use in fighting
I know you're getting slippery and sliding
Your fingers deeper and faster as I start describing
How she's glistening and her hands are gliding
She's following my lead and I'm guiding
Her to do sinful things now she's wiping
Her brow and I've found her most sensitive sport and start striking
Her chords, the melody of her harp is very inviting

Very Warm

I enjoy making you wet and very warm
In your hot holes let me create a firestorm
Taking a football team wearing your uniform
Drenching you with cum, a bukkake thunderstorm
Your holes are hot and many dicks swarm
Filling you until overflowing you're getting wet and very warm
You're a nasty, filthy cumbucket designed for porn
You're making being a nasty slut a new art form
You love looking in the camera as you perform
You're a filthy fucking whore the more I inform
You of your purpose it starts your nature as you transform
Being a receptacle for dicks makes you very wet and very warm

VIDEO VIXEN

Privately she's my super naughty video vixen
Putting it in her mouth, her pretty lips glisten
She starts undressing while I keep her attention
She does things secretly for me, she won't mention
Them to anyone else, she's a very hot video vixen
I'm definitely going to watch her hot video again
I love when she sucks things, putting it in
Her hot little mouth I love to listen
To the sounds coming out of my video vixen

WAKING

I love when your sensual parts start waking
Up you are so gorgeous, you're breathtaking
I'm whispering let my tongue start stimulating
Your desires until you start uncontrollably shaking
The hottest parts of you are slowly waking
As my tongue continues with fixating
On your beautiful neck, I hope to start making
You drip and that your body has been waiting
For delicious temptations, you are so fascinating
I strive to be better each day I am shaping
Your passions using my words to keep aiding
You in the most turned on creating
I'm in your head and slowly invading
It the feelings are so good and I keep trading
Up lighting a fire that is so blazing
Dream about me and imagine my tongue shaking
Your insides, open your legs as I continue waking

Weak Spot

With my mouth I start to exploit her weak spot
She could no longer fight temptation, she fought
Her urges but I know just how to make her very hot
She wants to be tied up with a firm knot
Making her fantasize about me nibbling her weak spot
With me she becomes far nastier than she ever thought
Possible as she removes her leggings and starts to squat
She's so eager for pleasure, everything that I've taught
Her nothing gets her warm like being caught
Touching herself always her pleasurable weak spot
She's frantically rubbing herself a lot
She's giving into temptation again, jackpot
I'm warming her insides like a teapot
She's melting thinking of my tongue onslaught
My tongue is teasing her weak spot

WEAKNESS

I'm incredibly vulnerable with her and my weakness
Is the winning combination with sweetness
When I express my desires with deepness
 That I desire only to bring her to completeness
She finds it impossible to resist, I've found her weakness
I'm her sunshine when life fills with bleakness
She knows with her I'm going to have success
Though I'm quite shy I don't see my meekness
As anything but opportunity to share uniqueness
When I'm smooth it evokes such sleekness
I'm an expert in bringing out her freakiness
I'm using my tongue to exploit her weakness

WET MIND

Nobody before had given her such a wet mind
She craves admiration, and I'm totally genuine
When I say you're breathtaking, you spellbind
My attention, the attention of a mastermind
Rather a master of creating sensational wet mind
When I mix creativity with one of a kind
Lyrics they are crafted with a specific design
To bring forth the diamond inside I combined
Creativity with desire as nothing like refined
Elegance makes her sparkle until others go blind
I want to touch all parts of her especially her hind
Quarters that makes her have such a wet mind

WRAPPING

There's a toy in her mouth and she starts wrapping
Her pretty lips around it, her lips are smacking
She keeps quickly touching herself she's grabbing
Herself more and more as her hands are attacking
Ripping open her present, destroying the wrapping
She feels the fire growing, the fire is happening
I'm in her mind and lap slowly lapping
It all up and she embraces the magic happening
She can't help but to quickly start jabbing
Her fingers inside as I am unmasking
Her deepest desires and slowly unwrapping
Her intricate desires this is gladdening
Her so much as my tongue starts wrapping